Winter Dance

MARION DANE BAUER   ILLUSTRATED BY RICHARD JONES

Houghton Mifflin Harcourt
Boston • New York

A single snowflake
       floats through the air,
spins,
       leaps,
settles
       on the nose
of a fine red fox.

"Winter is coming,"
says the fox.
"What should I do?"

"I can tell you what to do,"
  says a woolly caterpillar.
"Wrap yourself in a shiny chrysalis
  so you'll wake
  to a butterfly spring."
  And the woolly caterpillar
  crawls away
  to do just that.

"That won't do for me,"
  says the fox.
"I'm not meant to fly."

"I can tell you what to do,"
  a turtle calls.
"Tip your tail to the sky
      and swim

            down,

                              down,

                                    down

to bury yourself
in the
slick,
cool
mud."
And the turtle
does just that.

"That won't do for me,"
says the fox.
"Mud is much too . . . muddy!"

"Let me tell you what to do,"
whispers a bat.

"Zig
   and
zag
   and
swoop
   into a cave.

Then
hang
by
your
toes
and go to sleep."

And the bat
does just that.

"That won't do for me,"
says the fox.
"My toes would get tired."

Plop!
An acorn drops
from a tree.

"I can tell you what to do,"
chatters a squirrel.
"Gather, gather, gather.
Then quick,
quick,
hide everything away."
And he scampers off
to do just that.

"That won't do for me,"
says the fox.
"I don't even like acorns."

"We'll tell you what to do!"
geese honk from the sky.

"Flap your wings
and fly away
to warm days
and silky soft nights."

And—
     going,
          going,
               gone—
the geese do just that.

"That won't do for me,"
says the fox.
"I belong here in the forest."

A snowshoe hare
hops by in his new winter coat.
"I can tell you what to do,"
he says.
"Turn yourself white
to match the snow."

And the snowshoe hare,
who has done just that,
disappears into the whitening world.

"That won't do for me,"
says the fox.
"I love my red fur."

"I can tell you exactly what to do,"
says a great black bear.

"Curl beneath the roots
of a toppled balsam tree,
and tuck
all your growls
away."

And the great black bear
does just that.

"That won't do for me at all,"
says the fox.

"I'm not a bit sleepy!"

"Hush!"
the wind sighs.
"Hush!"

The fox
lies
down
on the forest floor
and puts his nose
between his paws.
The sun
slides
down
the blue bowl
of the sky.
"Hush!" the wind says
again.

The fox hushes.
More
snowflakes
land
on his
nose.

And then . . .
a whistle,
soft,
soft.

A white-tipped tail.
Golden eyes.

"I can tell you what to do,"
says a fine red fox,
bowing low.

"When a million snowflakes
fill the air,

twirling,

tumbling,

spinning,

waltzing,

you and I
join them."

"Of course!"
says the fox,
standing tall.
"Because that's what
we fine red foxes
do in winter.

Dance!"

For Katy, with love—M.D.B.

For Mike and Elizabeth—R.J.

Text copyright © 2017 by Marion Dane Bauer
Illustrations copyright © 2017 by Richard Jones

www.hmhco.com

The type was set in ITC Goudy Sans Std.

Library of Congress Cataloging-in-Publication Data is available.
ISBN 978-0-544-31334-7

Manufactured in Malaysia
TWP 10 9 8 7 6 5 4 3 2 1
4500664871